**PI
FOR 'M...**

# DEMAIN PUBLISHING

## Short Sharp Shocks!

Book 46: The Birthday Girl & Other Stories –
       Christopher Beck
Book 47: Crowded House & Other Stories - S.J.
       Budd
Book 48: Hand To Mouth – Deborah Sheldon
Book 49: Moonlight Gunshot Mallet Flame / A
       Little Death – Alicia Hilton
Book 50: Dark Corners - David Charlesworth

# Murder! Mystery! Mayhem!

Maggie Of My Heart – Alyson Faye
The Funeral Birds – Paula R.C. Readman
Cursed – Paul M. Feeney
The Bone Factory – Yolanda Sfetsos

# Beats! Ballads! Blank Verse!

Book 1: Echoes From An Expired Earth – Allen
Ashley
Book 2: Grave Goods – Cardinal Cox
Book 3: From Long Ago – Paul Woodward
Book 4: Laws Of Discord – William Clunie
Book 5: Fanged Dandelion – Eric LaRocca

# Weird! Wonderful! Other Worlds

Book 1: The Raven King – Liz Tuckwell
Book 2: The Wired City – Yolanda Sfetsos

# Horror Novels & Novellas

House Of Wrax – Raven Dane
A Quiet Apocalypse – Dave Jeffery
Cathedral (A Quiet Apocalypse Book 2) – Dave
Jeffery

The Samaritan (A Quiet Apocalypse Book 3) –
Dave Jeffery
And Blood Did Fall – Chad A. Clark
The Underclass – Dan Weatherer
Cheslyn Myre – Dan Weatherer
Greenbeard – John Travis
Tower Of Raven – Kevin M. Folliard
Little Bird – TR Hitchman
Society Place – Andrew David Barker

# General Fiction

Joe – Terry Grimwood
Finding Jericho – Dave Jeffery

# Science Fiction Collections

Vistas – Chris Kelso

# Horror Fiction Collections

Distant Frequencies – Frank Duffy
Where We Live – Tim Cooke
Night Voices – Paul Edwards & Frank Duffy

# Anthologies

The Darkest Battlefield – Tales Of WW1/Horror

# M.I.C.H.A.E.L.
## BY JESS DOYLE

# A SHORT SHARP SHOCKS!
# BOOK

# BOOK 52

To Die.

With love from

MoC4!

"Vengeance is in my heart, death in my hand, blood and revenge are hammering in my head."
- William Shakespeare, *Titus Andronicus*

# CONTENTS

# NO FLOWERS

<u>14th August, 1998</u>
At the crematorium, a spray of summer whites had been propped against the wall. Lilies, roses and gladioli with glossy, dark green foliage. Helen approached them at a pace, as though she intended to kick them. At the last second, she turned away and slumped against the red brick. She looked out over the dreary housing estate. Grey terraces under a drab sky.

A strange silence came over the place. An utter stillness, as though the world had paused. Helen wouldn't have been surprised to see a bird hanging in mid-air in that secret moment. A break out of time. She took a deep breath. She inhaled the sickly, sweet scent of lilies. That smell would always remind her of the funeral parlour. She had asked that no one send flowers. She'd wanted charity donations instead. He hadn't even liked flowers. She stared down at them as she lit a cigarette. Gladioli were the gaudiest of blooms. She imagined how they'd look by the end of the day, wilted and gloomy, much like herself.

There was a painful knot in Helen's stomach. She'd grieved once before, when her mother died. That time she'd felt it in her chest. As though she carried some enormous weight, like an anvil strapped up inside her rib cage. When she thought of it, she could still feel that weight. This time was different though. She could have believed that her insides had become tangled or maybe some major organ was missing altogether. She hadn't known she could grieve with her entire body.

She looked closer at the wreath as she puffed on her cigarette. There was a card among the blooms: *With deepest regret and heart-felt sympathies*. No name. Helen thought of the girlfriend. Conspicuously absent from the service. She was still hospitalised, gravely ill from the effect of shock, apparently. Unable to talk, to explain how it happened. Why Helen no longer had a son. Helen needed to know it all, every second in minute detail. And she couldn't bear to know any of it. She let her cigarette ash tumble onto the pristine white petals. There'd been rumours. Gossip about witchcraft and strange satanic rituals. Helen imagined the girlfriend would be pleased by that. It suited her image, black lipstick, pentacle tattoo and her first love burnt to death by black magic. Silent and secretive went with the attire.

Helen's head spun. The nicotine had hit hard. She hadn't smoked for almost nineteen years, until a week ago. The cigarette and the strong smell of lilies sent the knot in her stomach bolting upwards. Helen leaned against the wall and did not try to avoid the flowers as she brought up the coffee she'd managed to force down earlier. The snow-white blooms were splattered with milky brown bile.

Helen's throat was raw. The knot sat in her neck briefly before working its way back down to her belly. For a moment the smell of stale coffee overwhelmed even the strong perfume of the lilies. Helen thought bitterly that it was an improvement on the heavy floral fragrance. She heard a car door slam somewhere on the housing estate. Then a dog barked. The sound of the world stirring back into motion. The imagined frozen bird resumed its flight. Helen wiped her mouth on her sleeve, put out her cigarette with the sole of a vomit splattered shoe and entered the crematorium.

# ALWAYS SAY GOODBYE

6th August, 1998

Not all the candles were black. Some were a festive red and some sent the hefty scent of lavender drifting around the room. The array of candles stood on the windowsill, the bedside table and on top of the chest of drawers. When they seated themselves on the floor, the feeble flames illuminated only their faces. And the board.

"First, I have to tell you the rules." Emma's whisper cut into the serious silence and she frowned at her boyfriend's smirk.

"Mike. This is important," she hissed. "Listen carefully. First, if the planchette goes to the corners, or draws a figure of eight, that means the spirit is bad. End the conversation immediately. But always say goodbye. Never leave without saying goodbye. That's vital. And don't move your finger from the planchette during a conversation."

"The planchette's the pointy thing, right?" Mike nodded towards a triangular piece of wood with slightly curved edges like the head of an arrow.

"Right. And one more thing, don't ask when you're going to die."

"Why would I ask that?"

Emma shrugged. "Some people do. You got all that?"

Mike nodded. Emma placed the planchette on the board and they both put a fingertip to it.

"Hello. Is anyone there?"

M

"Don't mess around Mike. I've been wanting to try one of these for ages."

I

C

"It's not me."

H

"I swear, it isn't me."

A

E

L

"Alright, I believe you it's going too fast."

M.I.C.H.A.E.L.

M.I.C.H.A.E.L.

M.I.C.H.A.E.L.

They struggled to keep fingers on the planchette as it shot from one letter to another.

M.I.C.H.A.E.L.

M.I.C.H.A.E.L.

"Bit repetitive, isn't it?"

"Shut up. Hey, maybe it's a message for you."

"Is the message 'Michael?'"

"Say hello. It must want to talk to you."

"Hi."

"Introduce yourself. Go on."

Mike cleared his throat. "Hello. I'm Michael."

The planchette stopped. Then shivered; a tremor they felt in their fingertips. The flames of two dozen candles flickered as if a breeze had swept through the room.

"Whoa." Mike looked around the room with wide eyes.

Emma grinned excitedly. "Did you feel that?"

"Yes, and I didn't like it."

"Keep talking."

"I think we should stop."

"But it's just getting interesting. Please? Just ask what it wants."

"My name's Michael. Do you have something to say to me? Who are you? What do want?"

The planchette quivered. A slight shake at first. Then quickened to shuddering spasms. They struggled to keep a hold as it lifted and smacked down.

"Is this supposed to happen?" Mike asked.

"I don't know. I've never read about this happening before."

"I don't like it. I've had enough of this Em."

"Yeah, this isn't right. We have to say 'goodbye'." Emma said it loudly, clearly. To Mike, to herself and to who or whatever else might be listening. "Mike, you say goodbye too."

Mike opened his mouth to speak but only let out a grating groan. Pain shot up his arm like an electric current. He pulled away.

"Mike! You can't let go of the planchette. You have to say goodbye first."

Agony burrowed into his chest. He wheezed ugly, quaking rasps. His face reddened. His eyes bulged.

"Goodbye!" Emma shouted. "Goodbye! Goodbye!"

She reached for Mike. Put a hand to his arm and withdrew it fast. Her hand had blistered in an instant.

"Mike?"

He crashed forwards. His face smashed into the board with a hard whack. He clutched his throat as laboured breaths rattled from his chest. Emma leapt back, feeling heat radiate from Mike as though she were beside a furnace. Mike's entire body convulsed. His skin purpled and bubbled. A flame ignited from his torso. Emma screamed and ran from the room. A moment later Mike was engulfed.

# CUTRESS & PERRILL'S CURIOSITIES

3rd August, 1998

He found it in a junk shop. *Cutress & Perrill's Curiosities*. He'd walked past the place many times but he had never seen it open before. That day, though, the door stood open and the place smelled invitingly of old books. There was a calm hush to the place and no-one in sight. Mike paused for a moment and admired the dust motes that danced through sparse shards of sunlight. The walls were lined with books. They seemed old. Heavy leather-bound tomes. There were clusters of crammed tables crowding the room. He browsed the eclectic collection of trinkets and ornaments. There were stuffed animals, clocks, vases. He spotted a toby-jug like the one that his Grandma had owned, there was old china-ware, costume jewellery, and water-colour paintings in gilded frames.

Underneath a table he spotted a ouija board. He felt a jolt of excitement on seeing it. Emma was fascinated with the occult, it was just the sort of creepy, quirky gift she'd love. He knelt down to examine it. It looked old. *Perhaps it's haunted*. He smirked at the thought. It was heavily varnished, perfectly square and solid oak. The cursive lettering was engraved and finished in a fading grey. Otherwise it was fairly plain, no images of skulls, no scythe-wielding figure of death. He dusted it off with his sleeve. As he did, something clattered to the floor. A triangular shaped piece of wood.

"That goes with it."

Mike jumped.

The old man jumped with him. "Oh. Sorry lad. Didn't mean to scare you. That's the pointy thing. It's got a proper name, I don't recall it just now." He had wisps of grey hair and glasses so thick that it was difficult to make out his eyes.

"Um, thanks," Mike said as he picked up the triangle.

"It's an antique, that one. Victorian. From before they were even called ouija boards. They called them talking boards back then."

"Oh."

"It's probably even older than that, mind you. Reckon it's been repurposed as a Ouija board at some point. My guess is it was a side table before that. If you turn it over, you'll see. It has the remnants of legs in each corner."

"How much is it?"

"Yours for twenty pounds young man. As long as you promise me one thing." The old man gave him a stern look. "Don't use it."

Mike laughed.

"I'm serious."

"It's for my girlfriend. She's into this sort of thing."

"Well, don't let her use it either. Have it on display yes, that's fine. An ornament, that's all."

"I take it you're a believer then?"

"I never was." He shuffled closer to Mike and lowered his voice. "Then, well, my partner dragged me along to a séance," he whispered. "Damned thing's been following me ever since."

"Oh yeah? What damned thing's that then?"

"Shush, shush!" The old man frantically swept his arms up and down to silence him. "Thing is, it's my partner that brought this into the shop. I don't feel right about selling it but truth be told I'll be glad to see the back if it. You won't use it, will you?"

Mike made a show of placing a palm on his chest. "You have my solemn word, hand on heart."

The old man heaved a sigh of relief.

"So, what happened at this séance?" Mike asked as he fished in his pocket for cash.

The old man's eyes widened and he waved his arms around again. "It'll hear you!" he hissed. "It doesn't like me talking 'bout it, see? You tell your lady-friend, won't you? It's just an ornament."

"Of course. Thanks." Mike let the door swing shut behind him, an amused smile on his lips.

Perrill watched from the window as the young man walked away, struggling to hold the heavy oak board under his arm. He caught movement in the corner of his eye. A shadow, some stirring shade that ceased when he turned to face it. The cluttered shop seemed as it should be. Still he felt a heaviness in his chest.

His aged fingers clutched the counter as he felt a cool breath at his neck. Close to his ear came a low, indistinct whisper.

# A LETTER FROM BETHLEM HOSPITAL, 1902

<u>13th October, 1902</u>

My Dearest Friend,

No doubt you have been concerned for me. I know that I would be beside myself with worry had you been confined here. And so I write now to alleviate your concerns. Firstly, let me assure you that I am not confined to this place. Yes, it may be the case that doors and gates are locked. This is a matter of safety. It is also true that some security staff are conspicuous throughout the hospital. As it has been explained to me, they are simply here to protect patients and staff alike. That is what we are: 'patients' not 'detainees'. It is well-established between myself and the hospital staff that I am staying here on a purely voluntary basis. I may leave at any time I like and if at that time I find a locked door, it is merely a cautionary measure and I have only to discuss the matter with a member of staff.

Secondly, I must ask you to please be assured that the disagreeable rumours about this place are greatly exaggerated and its famously dark history is just that. History. Why, the place may have quite the reputation and it is indeed a heavy name to bear, 'Bedlam' as is it commonly called. The name may have followed the establishment but we are not even on the same site as that place of reported incarceration, torment and humiliation. Times have moved on. In fact, the hospital, in this modern age, is rather pleasant. As I write I am taking tea on the lawn with some of the more lucid and able female patients. Many on my ward have been committed for relatively minor disorders such as grief and insomnia. Or else they are here as a result of some moral crime, infidelity for instance.

I have made some unlikely friends. There are a surprising number of very pleasant and personable ladies. Though of course, these shan't be acquaintances I'll keep up once I've left this place and put this sorry episode behind me. There is scandal here, I will say. And in truth I rather enjoy overhearing the gossip amongst the staff. I dare say I'll have a story or two to relay over our much-missed afternoon teas. For instance, there is a young lady of my ward who has been committed as a nymphomaniac. Would you believe it: she's a vicar's daughter! Some of her tales are quite outrageous, honestly, I'm not at all sure that I'm bold enough to repeat them.

The truly insane patients, the incurable and the criminal, are confined to cells in the cellar for the large part of the day. We hear them spoken of but I have never seen any such lunatic about the hospital or its rather splendid grounds. We do hear them. Particularly when we are working in the laundry room which is also located in the cellar. Any words they utter are inaudible though, I could not tell you what the screams and moans are about. Some imagined horror, I suppose. Whatever the cause the sounds are certainly frightful. A tradition has grown of singing whilst in the laundry room. There are usually half a dozen of us at a time working the washing and we sing merry tunes, *All Things Bright and Beautiful* for instance, to drown out the terrible suffering of those poor souls.

I'll admit that some of the facilities here are a little lacking but the staff report promises of improvement from the management. Strangely, some of the inadequacies can be something of a blessing. For instance, the wind howls through the upper floors at night which are without windows. So many of the residents have sleeping problems it is a mercy that their remonstrations are, in effect, muted by the elements.

My dear friend, I am happy also to say that whatever accounts you may have heard of cruelty from the hospital staff are, in my experience, utter nonsense. My own treatment, for what has been termed 'hysteria', involves a programme of daily work, light exercise, some prayer and a certain amount of a new kind of 'talking therapy' which can be arduous but I certainly would not describe as unpleasant. I am expected to make a full recovery of course. It is only at night when I sometimes doubt it. We are not permitted lanterns or candles so that the nights are pitch black and as I have mentioned, full of noise. That's when I picture her face. Sometimes I even think I catch a voice, saying that name over and over. It is a relief when the moon is full and its soft light illuminates the ward. Then, I see instead the ghostly faces of patients painted with anguishes of their own. But I imagine that sounds rather grim to you and after all I am writing to reassure you.

All in all, my time here so far has been enormously beneficial, I would go so far as to say I am enjoying my stay. My days are full, stimulating and at times even joyful. I am increasingly finding that my mind rarely wanders back to that incident. At least, not until they turn out the lights.

Wishing you and yours much love.

"Revenge is the sweetest morsel to the mouth, that ever was cooked in hell."
 -Walter Scott, *The Heart of Midlothian*

# THE PARLOUR GAME

22nd August, 1902

Her screech tore through the stuffy parlour air, shocked and shrill. Sparrows that had gathered on the other side of the open window scattered in fright. Rebecca stared, wide eyed with surprise as her friend recovered.

"I'm sorry," Catherine giggled. "I had no idea it would move so fast."

"Really," Rebecca chuckled "It's just a silly game. What would you be like at a séance?"

"Oh, I daren't. Really. I'm sure this is enough mystery for me. Shall we try again?"

"If you think you can cope?" Rebecca said with a smile.

The ladies put their fingers back to the planchette and Catherine stifled a gasp as it shot to the 'M'.

Rebecca read the letters aloud as the planchette paused briefly on each, "M. I. C. H. A. E. L. Michael. It spells Michael."

The planchette continued moving.

"M. I. C. H. A. E. L. Michael again."

"I don't know a Michael. Do you?"

Catherine thought hard. "I can't think that I do."

M. I. C. H. A. E. L.

"Do you think it's going to say anything else?"

M. I. C. H. A. E. L.

"Do you know I've got a feeling it won't."

"Shall we play at cards instead?"

M. I. C. H. A. E. L.

"I was rather looking forward to this," Rebecca admitted.

"Everyone's talking about these boards. Everyone seems to be having such with them. But I agree, this is hardly exciting stuff. Perhaps we ought to..." She stopped.

"Rebecca? I say, are you quite alright, dear?"

Rebecca's eyes widened and her mouth gaped open. Catherine followed her friend's stunned stare past her own shoulder and found nothing. She returned her gaze to Rebecca, who seemed to have grown pale in seconds.

"Rebecca, dear. Are you quite alright? Rebecca?"

Rebecca did not respond. She beheld only the shadowy figure that lurked beside her friend. The apparition leaned over the board. A sleek curtain of black hair framed a lifeless and bloodied face. A tatty, old-fashioned black dress. Dark eyes. Wholly dark, like peep-holes into the abyss.

Rebecca did not have the wits to scream as the ghastly figure mutely mouthed the same word over and over again.

Michael

Michael

Michael

# SPRING FLOWERS

15th March, 1881

The new table was square, heavily varnished oak with tall, ornate legs that twisted to the floor like four thin turrets. Emily filled a white porcelain vase with water and placed it on the new parlour table. She added freshly cut daffodils. She'd picked them herself from the garden. The gardener would be unimpressed but daffodils were her favourite flowers and she loved to have them in the house. She'd cut a dozen, not quite in full bloom. In a day or two a vase of sunshine would sit on the new parlour table, cheering her every time she happened to glance in their direction. A little radiance to brighten the chill early spring and a promise of warmth and beauty to come as the days grew longer, warmer and lighter.

Within an hour the daffodils had closed up into tight buds once more, as if they had shut their eyes and tried to hide from the world. They bowed their heads as though in shame or pain. Later still they were drooped, wilted as though from thirst, though they had water enough and the light in the breakfast room was soft and cool.

Emily entered the breakfast room the next morning. She found that her daffodils had crumbled. They had dried and decayed as though they were long since dead. She found the water in the vase to be putrid, as if it had sat stagnant for an age.

Emily threw away the remains of her daffodils. She poured away the water, though its strong smell made her retch. She cleaned the vase. She poured fresh water and she picked tulips from the garden. They were buds, still tinged green but in a few days they'd be a riot of reds and yellows. Pretty flames to warm the chill spring days. By the afternoon their spear-like leaves were grey and shrivelled. The water was foul like a tiny swamp sat at the bottom of the vase.

Blackened and withered buds littered the breakfast room floor.

# THE CARPENTER

3rd September, 1880

The carpenter listed all that he had left. A single room that was both studio and living quarters. The clothes on his back. Enough to eat for the next few days. A single piece of solid oak. He had his hands. He had his eyesight and he had some small talent. He did not include his memories in the list, those were things he didn't wish to have amongst his belongings. Every morning began with the list.

He took his time at his work. He sawed. He chiselled. He carved. It would be a small piece but it would be fine quality. A parlour table for some wealthy family. The lady of the house would use it to display fine ornaments or vases of bright flowers. It would fetch enough to live for a month, maybe longer. And there would be enough left over for more lumber. More work to keep him occupied.

The carpenter's nights were long. He'd lie awake and curse the darkness that kept him from his work and barred him from busyness. He'd stare into the shadows and he'd breathe in the sawdust. He'd try not to think. As he drifted to sleep, he pushed pictures from his mind. Images of the family that poverty and illness stole from him. The woman and the son whose names he refused to even think. When sleep took him, nightmares engulfed him like flames on a funeral pyre. He dreamed of faces he had never seen and voices he had never before heard. There were jeers in the dark. Smoke and screams.

The carpenter woke breathless and perspiring. He yelled a name.

"Michael!"

He shouted it. And the name echoed around the room that was both studio and living quarters. Where the sawdust hung thick in the air. The name rang in his ears.

The carpenter had had a son once. His name was not Michael. The carpenter refused to bring his son's name to the forefront of his mind. He gasped and he wiped the sweat from his brow. He gulped the dusty air and he wondered why he dreamed of flames. Why wake to hear his own voice cry an unfamiliar name. Then the carpenter made a list. A single room that was both studio and living quarters. The clothes on his back. Enough to eat for the next couple of days. Work in hand to buy food and lumber. He had his hands. He had his eyesight and he had some small talent.

# THE FELL

8th May, 1778

"That's a monster of a tree," Mark's father whispered as he surveyed the enormous oak. As wide as it was tall, with branches that curled like immense beckoning fingers. The shadows it threw were deep and chilling and seemed to spread in every direction.

The men worked for hours, de-limbing and logging where the branches were too thin or twisted for lumber. But they said, despite its deformed appearance, the trunk was good, strong and sturdy. The long day had grown dark and the evening chill bit at Mark who had little hard work to warm him. It was his first time out with the men and his father had not let him hold a saw or an axe. He'd endured some teasing for his father's caution. He'd tried to busy himself as well as he could. He'd loaded the cart and he'd watched the horses. Two strong stallions, one chestnut, one black with a flash of white at its collar. They both were restless. Mark knew the horses well enough and he'd never seen them so spooked. The men remarked that they were good working horses, serious beasts not given to moods. They said that maybe the horses didn't like Mark. He sulked at that, he was good with horses, he knew it and took pride in it. He tried to comfort them with soft words and gentle hands but still the stallions stamped and grumbled.

When the time came to fell the oak's thick trunk Mark led the horses, cart still harnessed, well away. It would fall in the opposite direction but with them so unsettled it seemed wise to keep a good distance.

He heard the creak and the groan of wood. He heard the men cry out, the snap of neighbouring branches and crunch of foliage. He felt it. The crash. The rumble under his feet and the shake of the earth. Too close. The trunk had fallen in the wrong direction and far too close. The chestnut stallion reared. Strong legs and hard hooves struck the side of Mark's head. He was thrown to the ground. Knocked into the dirt in front of the black with the flash of white at its collar. They bolted together. Mark was trampled. Hard into the dust. The cart followed. Huge wheels over his young body. The weight of cart and timber pushed him further into the earth. He was broken. Mark heard his father's screams as the world went black.

# THE AUTUMN OAK

30th October, 1759

Laura kicked at leaves, delighted by their rustle and crunch. Her brother bounded around, climbed trees and stomped on fungus and Bella padded along contently, enjoying the smells of the woodland floor. At an oak tree Bella stopped. A low growl grew in her throat. Laura regarded the tree, all but bare of its blushed leaves, expecting to see a squirrel peering down from its ugly twisted branches.

"There's nothing there, silly." Laura went to pet the dog but Bella's haunches were up and her ears pinned back against her skull. Laura could see the whites of her eyes and the dog bared yellow teeth.

Laura took a step back, too young and trusting to be truly afraid of a pet but unnerved nevertheless.

"There's something wrong with Bella," Laura called to her brother.

He bounded past her and jumped at the tree. He caught a low branch and pulled himself up. Bella snarled and began circling the tree, giving it a wide and wary berth. Laura took another cautious step back and looked up at her brother. "Richard, something's wrong with Bella."

"Probably seen a squirrel," Richard said as he reached for another branch and tested its strength before climbing higher.

Laura peered further up into the tree. The sky was a bleached blue, almost white and the bare branches seemed black in contrast; dark, skeletal limbs against the pale heavens. There were no squirrels. There were no birds. The air was still despite the chill. No birdsong. No breeze to stir the dead leaves that littered the cold earth.

Bella whimpered. Laura understood the dog's fear though she could not have explained it. She looked up at her brother and found she was revolted to see him touch the sickening dark bark.

"Richard, I want to go back," she shouted up to him.

"In a minute."

"No, Richard, now." She bit down on her lip, realising her mistake. Her brother would take his time since she'd demanded he hurried. She tried to convince Bella instead. "Come on girl. Let's go." Her voice shook and she hoped that Richard had not heard. Bella ignored her, eyes focused on Richard. The dog paced and snarled.

Richard was ten feet from the ground. He spread out his arms to balance himself as he ventured along a long, winding branch. Below him Bella's snarls had turned to mad barks. He spun with a flourish, hoping to scare his sister.

In front of him, there stood a woman. Implausibly, where he had just stepped. Upright and still. She was dressed in black. Her face bloodied. Her eyes were dark and hollow. She moved forward. An effortless glide. He stepped back. His foot met nothing but air. He didn't manage a scream, the ground found him first. He fell backwards. His head struck the hard earth. The sound was that of unearthly crunch of bone. It was echoed only by Bella's howl and Laura's scream.

# THE OAK TREE

<u>29<sup>th</sup> August, 1625</u>

The tiny haze of a chill breath hangs a moment at the squirrel's mouth. The dirt under-paw is curious. It's not just cold. There is something akin to motion, not unlike the quake in the air before a storm. Dark clouds sweep through her memory and she recalls winter's icy touch. She pictures the trees around her festooned with frost and a snowy shroud covering the earth. But the leaves have not begun to fall. There is green all about her, not reds and yellows. Autumn's warning signs are yet to show. It is too early to feel winter's raw embrace. She shudders. Her tiny paws prickle upon the peculiar earth. She drops her acorn. She flees.

But a little sunlight falls on that strange place. The acorn takes root. It weaves delicate vines into the ground. The dainty green threads reach deep down into the dirt. They find something. A body. Charred and rotting. The roots coil their way around bones. Suck nutrients. Grow wide and strong. The roots swallow the skeleton. They are one.

The acorn becomes an oak. She grows tall and strong. She eclipses the daylight so that nothing else will grow. Her branches are crooked and the shadows she throws are true dark and savagely cold. Birds do not nest in her jagged branches. Mice and squirrels do not harvest her bitter seeds. Even the relentless ivy with little need of light turns its tendrils and creeps away.

Few venture near. No one hears in the dead of night when the wind stirs her leaves and she whispers a name into the dark.

# THE GRAVEDIGGER

<u>14th June, 1621</u>

He collects the remains in a burlap sack. He's never used a sack before but there is no coffin and no one has thought to offer a box. What's left is charred and broken. It breaks all the more as he slings the sack into his wheelbarrow. He knows better than to take it to the churchyard. When he pauses beside a field a neighbour is there to chastise him in seconds.

"Not round here. We won't have her round here," the burly man shouts.

The gravedigger scowls. No one's thought to tell him what to do with her. "Where would you have me put her?" he spits.

"I don't care where you put her, just so long as it's away from here."

The gravedigger grumbles and spits again.

The burly man begins to walk away then stops and says "Put her in the woods. That place is already tinged with evil."

The gravedigger doesn't admit his loathing of the woods. He deals in dirt and death. He cannot confess how he is unsettled by the dark, by the tall shadows thrown by ancient trees. By rustling in the undergrowth.

He's anxious as he ventures into that old place. He finds a clearing of sorts, where a little light fights its way through the green canopy. Here, exhausted bluebells hang their heads and wait for death.

A strange feeling as he digs. Do eyes bore into him as he works? He seeks to expel the silence and the shiver down his spine. He mutters the prayer that he knows, hoping that voicing it might protect him from whatever evil lurks in the woods.

"Our Father, who art in Heaven. Hallowed be thy name." He mutters it to himself, concentrating on the words as the spade hits the earth. Did he hear a whisper at his back? He drowns it out.

"Thy kingdom come, thy will be done, on earth as it is in Heaven." A rustle in the bushes.

"Give us this day our daily bread and forgive us our trespasses." He lifts his head in time to see a blackbird dash away. A blur of black and a glimpse of amber. But he does not laugh at himself. The feeling has not passed.

"As we forgive those that trespass against us." He digs the shallowest grave. Barely a foot into the dark earth.

"Lead us not into temptation." He throws in the sack.

"But deliver us from evil." He does not pause to recover himself. He begins at once to cover bone and burlap with soil.

"For thine is the kingdom." A murmur. Right behind him. His body freezes but his voice keeps going. "The power and the glory." He shuts his eyes. "For ever and ever." He breathes hard and fast. "Amen."

He thinks about starting the prayer again but the first line, uttered so often is suddenly missing from his mind. He tries to summon a picture of the blackbird. Black and amber, its sharp eyes searching the woodland floor for worms. He tries to picture a squirrel or even a rat. The only image that comes to mind is the witch, the look of anguish on her face as the flames consumed her.

The sound has stopped but the gravedigger has a strong sense that he is not alone. He finds a scent in the air. Smoke. He feels no heat but he smells smoke as clearly as he had the previous night when he'd watched the fire take her.

He raises to his full height slowly. Opens his eyes. He takes a deep shuddering breath and whips around fast, spade in hand. She is there. Her eyes empty. Black. Her hair sleek and dark. Blood running down her face and her dark dress smouldering like a newly extinguished flame. The gravedigger drops the spade. He falls. He topples back against the witch's shallow grave. She regards him with her empty eyes. Then she is gone. Vanished like dispersed smoke. He staggers to his feet. He flees. He leaves his spade and his wheelbarrow. He never returns for them.

"Thou shalt not suffer a witch to live."
- Exodus 22:18

# THE WITCH

## 13th June, 1631

It was dusk when they led her from the church. The heavens, painted a pastel pink and the evening's shadows, tall and slim. A calm breeze played with her loose dark hair and brought the sound of the braying crowd to her long before they reached it.

Her hands had been bound tight behind her back. So tight that she'd lost sensation in her fingers. The throng was thick, surely more than just the villagers. Had they come from neighbouring parishes to watch? How far had the tale spread? They led her through them, the mob that roared for retribution. They dragged her along the ground when her legs gave way through fear. The jeers were too many and too loud for her to heed. Or to pick out a voice of one that rejoiced to see her burn. Faces lurched at her. She knew many of them. Neighbours who'd once greeted her warmly now half-crazed with rage. Strangers too, all united in their revulsion. Spit hit her full in the face. Stones collided with her body. A jagged rock, flung with force, flew above the rabble and caught the top of her head. Blood ran down her face and into her eyes. With her hands bound behind her she could do nothing to wipe them clear so she was hauled, half blind to the pyre.

They tied her tight to the stake, the ropes cut in so that every breath was a struggle. She hoped her body might lose sensation as her hands had done. A torch was thrown down and the roar of a jubilant crowd echoed the roar of fire as the pyre ignited fast. She cried out then but her shrieks and pleas for mercy were met with only glee.

Heat filled her lungs and pressed against her flesh. She screamed long and raw when her dress caught a flame and she first felt the cruel touch of fire on her skin. The crowd delighted in her agony.

She fought to open her eyes, to see, so that she might appeal to someone, anyone. Her vision was dulled with pain and with blood and smoke. The villagers were nothing but dancing shadows beyond the flames.

But one stood closer and stood still. One neither triumphant nor anguished. Through the haze of red and black, she knew him. His face was hard, no grief and no joy. He stood and he watched his sister burn.

When finally she perished, she did so with her brother's name on her lips.

# THE WITNESS

5th June, 1631

His sister whispers prayers into the night. He hears them in the small hours when she believes the family asleep. Hissed hymns into darkness for a beloved devil. Often her words are strange, a language unfamiliar to his ear. When he hears her ungodly worship his blood runs cold, he cannot move a single muscle and he can barely draw breath. He knows it is not fear that paralyses him but some power summoned by her dark words. The same magic binds his voice all the day. He may speak but not of her. And not of her wicked deeds. Nothing of what he has witnessed. For so long it's been as though his tongue were tied against telling. Some wicked spell that at last grows weak.

Now he speaks of the horrors he has seen. He tells of demons made of shade and smoke that dance about her. He has seen fiends reach out and touch her in ways that sicken him. Ways that give her ungodly pleasure. Lately such a creature brought her a token of its work for her. A shadow, coloured black and purple like a bruise and with the shape of a goat. Grotesque, with its twisted horns and how it stood on its hind quarters. He saw it present her with a memento: a handful of golden hair and a bloodied rock. It can be found now beneath her bed where she stowed her wicked trinket.

Now that her spell has broken, he at last bears witness. And at last he can cry. He cries for what his sister has become. He grieves the innocent little girl that she once was but is now just a distant memory. He weeps for what she has taken from him. From them all. His tears fall hardest for the life taken by her imp for jealousy's sake. Beauty and youth dashed out by his sister's cold heart. Were only that his tongue had not been bound as it was, what horrors might have been prevented. But only now can he speak. Only now can he cry. And now God's justice may be done.

# THE SILENCE

3rd June, 1631

No one comes. Anne does not come. The bright, beautiful girl in the next cottage. Every morning she knocks on Margaret's door. And every morning Margaret refuses her help. Margaret doesn't want anyone to fetch her water, to buy her bread, to help with the few vegetables that still grow in her little garden. She has all she can ask of the day because Anne has come into her cottage like sunshine bursting through cloud. Margaret remembers her own mother being just the same. There was nothing you could do for her but offer her a smile. Margaret picks up her stick and hobbles out of the door. She means to knock on Anne's door, but she finds it askew.

She knows by the silence. A memory comes to Margaret. It plays over in her mind as she stands at Anne's door. Such a long time ago, she was younger than Anne is now, more a girl than a woman. She remembers waking on that clear spring morning, she remembers the soft light flooding the little cottage. But it was later than she'd usually wake. Her mother had not woken her. And she heard it. A stillness that meant no other breathed that same air. This very same silence. That morning she had found her mother, cold and stiff in her bed.

Margaret knows this silence. She knows what it means. She peers a little way through the door. Just enough to catch sight of Anne's feet, still booted. Enough to know that her body lies across the kitchen floor. Margaret does not enter the cottage. She has seen enough death in her long life. Someone else can look upon the girl's lifeless body. They can discover the dent in her skull and the awful gash that has turned her golden hair blood-red. Margaret has seen enough.

# A FISTFUL OF HAIR

<u>2nd June, 1631</u>

He still holds the rock in his hand. He had intended to sling it at her door. It's as big as his fist and it's grown warm with his touch so that holding it has begun to feel natural. Now he stands in front of her. In Anne's kitchen, wondering how he got here, when he decided to barge his way in. He remembers hearing her gentle singing from outside. Her voice light and full of joy. He remembers feeling heat rush to his head. But charging in to the little cottage? That moment is missing from memory.

A moment passes as they regard each other. She sees the hurt and the fury etched on his face. She sees the rock in his fist too. He sees her confusion and her fear. There's anger there too. Outrage that he stands before her with a rock in his fist.

He sees her eyes flick around the room, to the door behind him, to the knife sat on the table. She lurches for the knife. He catches her by her hair before she can put a finger to it. She doesn't scream. He puzzles over that later. She might have brought neighbours running with a scream. But she only sounds his name in a choked whisper: "Michael".

He brings the rock down on her head. Hard and fast. She falls to the floor like a sack of potatoes. Leaving him with a fistful of golden hair in one hand. A warm and bloody rock in the other.

"You have witchcraft on your lips."
- William Shakespeare, *Henry V*

# THE SECRET

2<sup>nd</sup> June, 1631

The girls swing their baskets as they walk. They do this often, off into the woods to forage. They'll come back with berries and nuts, sometimes herbs and mushrooms. Most won't go into the woods. They're old and dark and most are frightened. But Mary and Anne go often. Michael listens to their idle chatter as he follows them. His sister Mary and her friend Anne, the girl he's chosen for himself. He follows them into the woods, though the brambles snatch at his clothes and hidden rocks conspire to trip him. He keeps up, his stumbling disguised by the birds and the breeze. He stalks part for the joy of watching his love, part for the pleasure of antagonising his sister. He'll scare them, jump out at them where the woods are darkest.

Their voices become low. Whispered secrets. Michael is too far to hear but he can see the gentle smile between them. Anne takes Mary's hand. Perhaps she is frightened of the woods after all. But then she raises Mary's hand to her lips and plants a gentle kiss on her knuckles. Her lips linger for a long moment. It is difficult for Michael to see but he imagines her eyes are closed. Mary reaches for Anne and her fingers become lost in her long golden hair. They kiss deeply, so lost in each other they do not hear Michael's anguished groan.

# GOD'S WORK

<u>20th May, 1631</u>

The sermon is an assault on the damned. Sinners feel each word like a punch in the chest.

"Be sober. Be vigilant. Because your adversary the devil, as a roaring lion, walketh about, seeking whom he may devour."

He lets his congregation soak it up, saturate in it like meat steeping in marinade. He casts his eyes down over them; studies his sombre congregation. Someone shuffles their feet and he searches for them, his eyes darting vulture-like for the guilty. He wonders if any of them have not fallen prey to Satan's wicked will. Is there a soul in this parish not submerged in darkness?

"Have no fellowship with the unfruitful works of darkness, but rather *reprove* them." He makes the last words sound hopeful, allowing his commanding voice to soften, just a little. It's an offer of redemption. He is a good shepherd; fear is his crock and he steers his flock towards the light. Away from all that is dark and unholy. This is God's work.

A young man sits enthralled by the sermon, captivated by the almighty's emissary; every word is a revelation. He wears the stunned look of a man emerging from darkness into brilliant light.

"*Reprove them*." The preacher repeats the words and smiles kindly at his new disciple.

"I have love in me the likes of which you can scarcely imagine and rage the likes of which you would not believe. If I cannot satisfy one, I will indulge in the other."
- Mary Shelley, *Frankenstein*

# IN THE WOODS

<u>18th April, 1622</u>

The woods hold no fear for them. It is a place for secrets and it feels like home to Anne and Mary. They know beauty everywhere they look. The deep green ivy that sprawls underfoot; the lichen littered bark of gnarly, ancient trees; rocks embossed with moss, and the subtle scent of wild garlic. They listen to a blackbird's bright chorus as they walk, deeper into the woods.

At the clearing they throw down their baskets and the pretence of foraging. They step into the bluebells and it feels like wading into a serene sea. Anne reaches to pluck a dandelion seed that has settled in Mary's dark hair and they watch it float away; a fragment of a wish caught on the breeze. Anne wonders whose wish since she holds her own in her hands; Mary's fingers woven around her own and the smile in her dark eyes, black and brilliant like beaming obsidian. Dappled sunshine finds its way through the green canopy, it makes Anne's hair glow gold, as though she's framed by a shining halo.

Their mouths meet and the world melts away.

## THE END

# BIOGRAPHY

Jess Doyle is a writer of horror and dark fiction from North Wales. Her stories have been published in The Cabinet of Heed, Hypnopomp Magazine, Coffin Bell, Horror Scribes, Zeroflash and Idle Ink.

Her short story *A Little Something for the Dead* was published by <u>Bone and Ink Press</u> and was nominated for 'Best of The Net'.

Her short story *Luna Too* was recently published in The Third Corona Book of Horror Stories.

You can find Jess on Twitter as @jcdoyley

## ADRIAN BALDWIN (COVER ARTIST)


Adrian is a Mancunian now living and working in Wales. Back in the 1990s, he wrote for various TV shows/personalities: Smith & Jones, Clive Anderson, Brian Conley, Paul McKenna, Hale & Pace, Rory Bremner (and a few others). Wooo, get him! Since then, he has written three screenplays—one of which received generous financial backing from the Film Agency for Wales. Then along came the global recession which kicked the UK Film industry in the nuts. What a bummer! Not to be outdone, he turned to novel writing—which had always been his real dream—and, in particular, a genre he feels is often overlooked; a genre he has always been a fan of: Dark Comedy (sometimes referred to as Horror's weird cousin). *Barnacle Brat* (a dark comedy for grown-ups), his first novel won Indie Novel of the Year 2016 award; his second novel *Stanley Mccloud Must Die!* (more dark comedy for grown-ups) published in 2016 and his third: *The Snowman And The Scarecrow* (another dark comedy for grown-ups) published in 2018. Adrian Baldwin has also written and published a number of dark comedy short stories. He designs book covers too—not just for his own books but for a growing number of publishers. For more information on the award-winning author, check out:

https://adrianbaldwin.info/

# DEMAIN PUBLISHING

To keep up to-date on all news DEMAIN (including future submission calls and releases) you can follow us in a number of ways:

BLOG:
www.demainpublishingblog.weebly.com

TWITTER:
@DemainPubUk

FACEBOOK PAGE:
Demain Publishing

INSTAGRAM:
demainpublishing

Printed in Great Britain
by Amazon

77710107R00051